HeartFelt
STORIES

HeartFelt Stories began with a dream fueled by
enthusiasm that lives in the very heart of our souls.
We've given life to our dream by creating a collection of stories
and characters we hope will bring a smile
to your face and have a permanent place in your heart.
Thank You!

...en Our Books And You Will Find We're Touching Hearts And Shaping Minds

Published by IdeaStream Consumer Products, LLC
Story created and written by Denise Bloom/David Rastoka
Illustrations by Kimo Tenorio
Design by Eric Klosky

For more information, contact:
Heartfelt Stories, LLC / 5767 Kempton Run Drive, Columbus, OH 43235
www.heartfeltstoriesllc.com

Library of Congress Controll Number: 2010920427
Library of Congress Cataloging-in-Publication Date is available
ISBN-13: 9780977811366 / ISBN-10: 0-9778113-6-0

10 9 8 7 6 5 4 3 2

TAKE IT TO HEART

Yesterday everything seemed right
an afterschool snack, a kiss goodnight.
Then suddenly life seems unfair,
so many questions...unanswered prayers.
Okay, why me? You want to scream
and cry and stomp and let off steam.
That's okay! Don't keep it in,
letting it out is where you begin.
Even when you're dealt a lousy hand
and it seems like no one understands,
there's something you have deep down inside
that will be there when the tears have dried.
Courage is what that "something" is called,
it's there no matter how hard you fall.
Healing will happen; take it day by day.
People who care aren't far away.
That inner strength will help you begin
to hold memories in your heart and find your grin,
and if things get dark and you've lost your sight,
that love in your heart will be your light!

–Denise Bloom

The Ohio State University Comprehensive Cancer Center – Arthur G. James
Cancer Hospital and Richard J. Solove Research Institute
has committed to helping children who are in crisis due to the
serious illness or death of a loved one.

For more information or to make a donation to the
Healing Journey for Children visit:
www.cancer.osu.edu/go/children.com

CLICKITY CLICK!

Then he heard something coming
with a clickity click,
as he approached the
beautiful red heels,
he thought, *man...that was quick!*

Then he got closer to Lil' Brutus,
moved right in with a strut,
leaned in tightly and whispered,
"Boy, you're a football nut!"

**Brutus now had direction
and was filled with ambition.
It was on that November day
that his quest became a mission!**

When he rounded the corner
he stopped right in his tracks,
for he could see the Horseshoe Stadium,
now there was no turning back!

Brutus took a deep breath
and in a flash he had no fear
r he thought of friends and family
who helped to get him here.

HeartFelt STORIES

Heartfelt Stories Is A Series Of Children's Books
That Are Geared Towards Teaching Children
Life Lessons And Core Values.

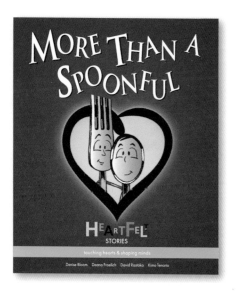

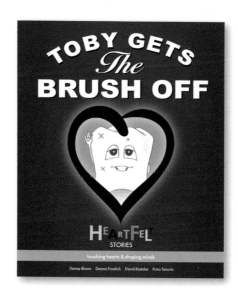

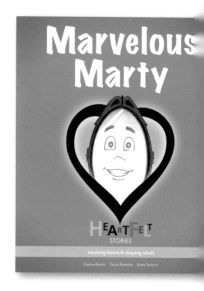

MORE THAN A SPOONFUL

Little Spooner thinks the peas are greener on the other side of the plate. This adorable story of two friends, Spike and Spooner, takes you on a journey of self-discovery. More Than A Spoonful teaches some valuable lessons: Love yourself for who you are, recognize what you can do, be proud and be happy, for you're special too!

TOBY GETS THE BRUSH OFF

Does brushing and flossing make your kids stick out their tongues? If so, Toby Gets The Brush Off, with its whimsical text and fun illustrations, is the book for you! Read how Toby, the molar, begs for more attention because Ms. Toothbrush is always rushing. Come along with Toby to the dentist and enjoy his healthy turn around. This story sends a simple but important message; take care of your teeth and they'll always be there for you.

MARVELOUS MARTY

Sometimes it's tough to see the g in ourselves when we are so focu on our imperfections. Marvelous Marty, a story of a mirror, helps all to take a second glance and he teaches us to be kind to other Marty the mirror hangs in the lob of a grand hotel where he eventu ally helps onlookers to see things his way, with encouragement of h friend Freddy the ficus tree. This book encourages children to like themselves for who they are and it teaches them that beauty is not measured on good looks but rath doing good deeds.